This **F**rog book belongs to:

....

This paperback edition first published in 2014 by Andersen Press Ltd.

20 Vauxhall Bridge Road, London SW1V 2SA.

First published in Great Britain in 1994 by Andersen Press Ltd.

Published in Australia by Random House Australia Pty.,

20 Alfred Street, Milsons Point, Sydney, NSW 2061.

Colour separated in Switzerland by Photolitho AG, Zürich.

Printed and bound in China by Foshan Zhaorong Printing Co., Ltd.

10 9 8 7 6 5 4 3 2 1

British Library Cataloguing in Publication Data available.

ISBN 978 1 78344 142 6

Frog

is Frightened

Max Velthuijs

Andersen Press

Frog was very frightened. He was lying in bed,
and he could hear strange noises everywhere.
There was a creaking in the cupboard and a
rustling under the floorboards.
"Somebody is under my bed," thought Frog.

He jumped out of bed and ran through the dark woods until he reached Duck's house.

"How nice of you to come and see me," said Duck.
"But it is rather late. I'm about to go to bed."
"Please, Duck," said Frog. "I'm frightened.
There's a ghost under my bed."

"Nonsense," laughed Duck. "There's no such thing."
"There is," said Frog. "The woods are haunted as well."
"Don't be frightened," said Duck. "You can stay with me. I'm not afraid."
And they huddled into bed together. Frog cuddled Duck's warm body and wasn't frightened any more.

All of a sudden they heard a scratching noise on the roof.
"What was that?" asked Duck, sitting up with a jolt.
The next moment they heard a creaking on the stairs.
"This house is haunted too!" shouted Frog. "Let's get
out of here."
And they ran out into the woods.

Frog and Duck ran as fast as they could.

They felt there were ghosts and scary
monsters everywhere.

Eventually they reached Pig's house and, gasping for breath, they hammered on the door.
"Who is it?" asked a sleepy voice.
"Please, Pig, open the door. It's us," shouted Frog and Duck.

"What's the matter?" asked Pig angrily. "Why have you woken me up in the middle of the night?"
"Please help us," said Duck. "We're terrified. The woods are full of ghosts and monsters."
Pig laughed. "What nonsense. Ghosts and monsters don't exist. You know that."
"Well, look for yourself," said Frog.

Pig looked out of the window, but she couldn't see anything unusual.
"Please, Pig, may we sleep here? We're so scared."
"O.K.," said Pig. "My bed is big enough. And I am never frightened. I don't believe in all that rubbish."

So there they were, all three of them together in
Pig's bed.
"This is nice," thought Frog. "Nothing can happen now."
But they couldn't sleep. They listened to all the
strange, frightening noises in the woods.
This time, Pig heard them too!

But luckily the three friends could comfort
each other. They shouted out that they
were not scared – that they weren't afraid
of anything. Eventually they fell asleep
exhausted.

Next morning, Hare went to visit Frog. The door was wide open and Frog was nowhere to be seen. "This is strange," thought Hare.

Duck's house was also empty.
"Duck, Duck, where are you?" shouted Hare. But there was no answer. Hare was very worried. He thought something terrible must have happened.

Terrified, he ran through the woods looking
for Frog and Duck. He looked and looked
but there was no trace of his friends.
"Perhaps Pig will know where they are,"
he thought.

Hare knocked on Pig's door. There was no answer.
It was very quiet. He looked in through the window
and there he saw his three friends lying in bed,
fast asleep. It was ten o'clock in the morning!
Hare knocked on the window.

"Help! A ghost!" shouted the three friends.
Then they saw that it was Hare.

Pig unlocked the door and they all ran outside.
"Oh, Hare," they said. "We were so frightened.
The wood is full of ghosts and scary monsters."
"Ghosts and monsters?" said Hare surprised.
"They don't exist."

"How do you know?" said Frog angrily. "There was one under my bed."

"Did you see it?" asked Hare quietly.

"Well, no," said Frog. He hadn't *seen* it but he had heard it. They talked about ghosts and monsters and other ghastly things for a long time.

Pig made some breakfast.
"You know," said Hare. "Everyone is frightened
sometimes."
"Even you?" asked Frog, surprised.

"Oh yes," said Hare. "I was very frightened this morning when I thought you were lost."
There was a silence.

Then everyone laughed.
"Don't be ridiculous, Hare," said Frog. "You have nothing to fear. We are always here."

Max Velthuijs's twelve beautiful stories about **Frog** and his friends first started to appear twenty five years ago and are now available as paperbacks, e-books and apps.

9781783441440 9781783441532 9781783441501 9781783441426

9781783441471 9781783441457 9781783441525 97811783441433

9781783441518 9781783441495 9781783441488 9781783441419

Max Velthuijs (Dutch for Field House) lived in the Netherlands, and received the prestigious Hans Christian Andersen Medal for Illustration. His charming stories capture childhood experiences while offering life lessons to children as young as three, and have been translated into more than forty languages.

**'Frog is an inspired creation – a masterpiece of graphic simplicity.'
GUARDIAN**

'Miniature morality plays for our age.' IBBY